Dear Parent:
Your child's love of reading

Every child learns to read in a different way and at his or her own speed. You can help your young reader improve and become more confident by encouraging his or her own interests and abilities. You can also guide your child's spiritual development by reading stories with biblical values and Bible stories, like I Can Read! books published by Zonderkidz. From books your child reads with you to the first books he or she reads alone, there are I Can Read! books for every stage of reading:

SHARED READING
Basic language, word repetition, and whimsical illustrations, ideal for sharing with your emergent reader.

BEGINNING READING
Short sentences, familiar words, and simple concepts for children eager to read on their own.

READING WITH HELP
Engaging stories, longer sentences, and language play for developing readers.

READING ALONE
Complex plots, challenging vocabulary, and high-interest topics for the independent reader.

ADVANCED READING
Short paragraphs, chapters, and exciting themes for the perfect bridge to chapter books.

I Can Read! books have introduced children to the joy of reading since 1957. Featuring award-winning authors and illustrators and a fabulous cast of beloved characters, I Can Read! books set the standard for beginning readers.

A lifetime of discovery begins with the magical words **"I Can Read!"**

Visit www.icanread.com for information on enriching your child's reading experience.
Visit www.zonderkidz.com for more Zonderkidz I Can Read! titles.

Ask and it will be given to you.
—*Matthew 7:7*

ZONDERKIDZ

Little David Sings for the King

Requests for information should be addressed to:

Zonderkidz, *Grand Rapids, Michigan 49530*

Library of Congress Cataloging-in-Publication Data

Bowman, Crystal.

Little David sings for the king / by Crystal Bowman ; illustrated by Frank Endersby.
p. cm. – (I can read. Level 1) (David series)
ISBN 978-0-310-71711-9 (softcover)
[1. Mice—Fiction. 2. Size—Fiction. 3. David, King of Israel—Fiction. 4. Christian life—Fiction.]
I. Endersby, Frank, ill. II. Title.
PZ7.B68335Li 2010
[E]—dc22 2008008371

Editor: Mary Hassinger
Art direction: Jody Langley

Printed in China

10 11 12 13 14 15 /SCC/ 6 5 4 3 2 1

I Can Read!™ BEGINNING 1 READING

Little David Sings for the King

story by Crystal Bowman

pictures by Frank Endersby

Little David sat under a tree.

He watched his big brothers.

They played in the field.

They ran races.

David was the little brother.

"May I run with you?" asked David.

"You are too small to play with us,"

said his big brother Pete.

David counted the birds,

"One, two, three, four."

Four birds sat high in the tree.

The birds sang songs to God.

David went to his room.

He sat by the window.

He played songs on his harp.

He sang songs to God
just like the birds.
The songs made him feel happy.

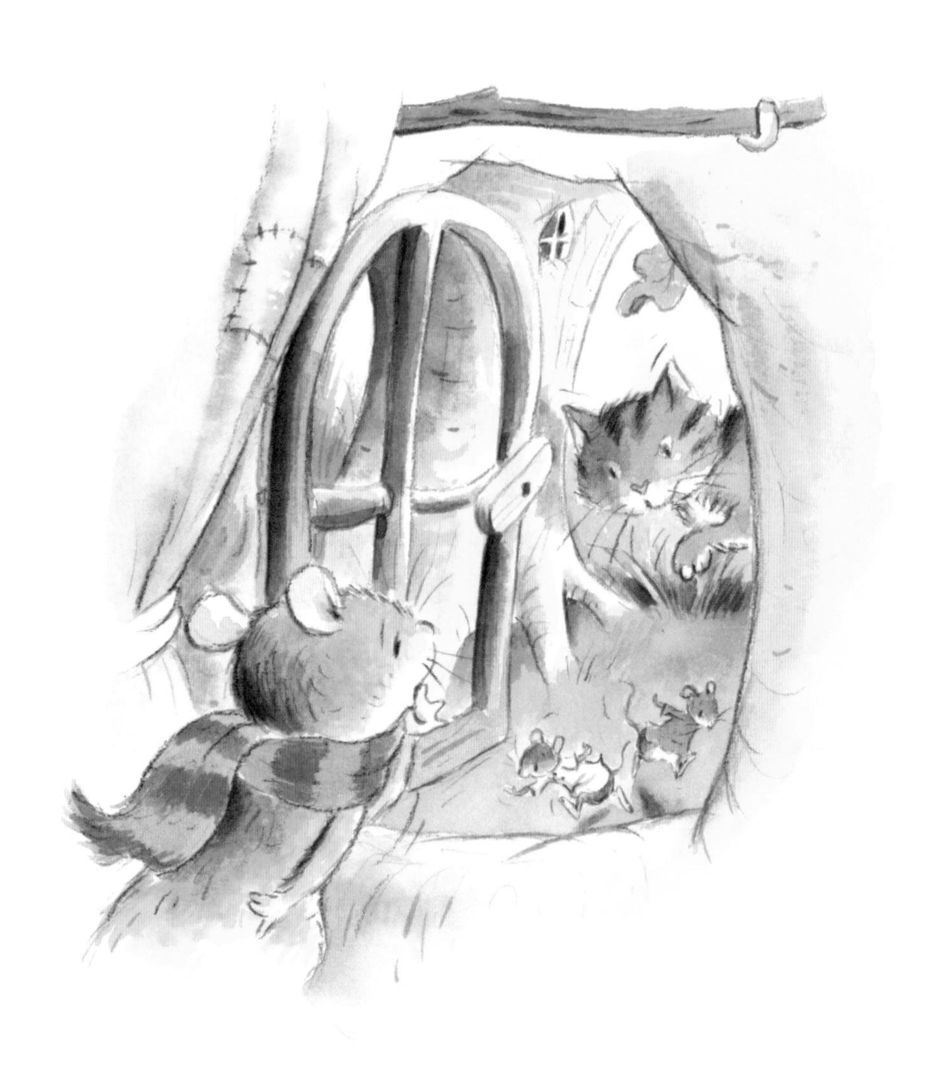

Then David saw a big cat outside.

His brothers were afraid.

They ran and hid in the bushes.

But God helped David to be brave.

“Go away!” yelled David.

The cat ran far away.

David laughed and laughed.

David's brothers came inside.

"We want a snack," said Josh.

David put bowls on the table.

He put milk and cheese in the bowls.

David's brothers sat in big chairs.

David sat in a little chair.

David said a prayer to God.

"Thank you for our food," he said.

Knock! Knock! Knock!

A very tall mouse was at the door.

David's father opened the door.

“Who are you?” asked David’s father.

“The king of mice sent me here,”

said the very tall mouse.

"Come in," said David's father.

The tall mouse came into the house.

"The king is very sad," he said.
"He wishes to find someone
who can make him happy."

“I have many sons,”

said David’s father.

"They are big and strong.
Maybe they can help the king."

The tall mouse looked at

David's brothers.

Then he looked at little David.

“The king wants David
to play songs for him,” he said.
“Please let David come with me.”

David's father was happy.

He said, "David may go with you to play for the king."

Little David took his harp.

He said good-bye to his brothers.

He rode in a big cart.

Two white dogs pulled the cart

to where the king lived.

David played his harp for the king.

"Play more songs," said the king.

David played many more songs.

Then the king was happy again.

David was the smallest mouse
in his family.
But God helped David do big things.